DAVE KEANE

Joe Sherlock

KID DETECTIVE

Case #000001:
The Haunted Toolshed

■ HarperCollins*Publishers*

Library of Congress Cataloging-in-Publication Data
Keane, David, date
  The haunted toolshed / by David. J. Keane.—1st ed.
    p.   cm.— (Joe Sherlock, kid detective ; #000001)
  Summary: A super-sleuth fourth grader solves the case of a
neighbor's haunted toolshed.
  ISBN-10: 0-06-076189-x (trade bdg.)
  ISBN-13: 978-0-06-076189-9 (trade bdg.)
  ISBN-10: 0-06-076188-1 (pbk. bdg.)
  ISBN-13: 978-0-06-076188-2 (pbk. bdg.)
  [1. Neighbors—Fiction. 2. Ghosts—Fiction. 3. Mystery and
detective stories.] I. Title.
PZ7.K2172Caj 2006   2005014898
[Fic]—dc22   CIP
                                                              AC

Typography by Christopher Stengel
1 2 3 4 5 6 7 8 9 10
❖
First Edition

For Christine, who always believed
—D.K.

Contents

My name is Joe Sherlock.

But almost everybody just calls me Sherlock. Never Joe.

In fact, most people around here think I squirted into this world without a proper first name attached.

But for me, Sherlock is the perfect fit, like a worn-out pair of sneakers that you just love but your mom throws out anyway, because she's simply horrified that one of her friends might actually see you wearing them.

So what's so great about having a name like a smelly old pair of sneakers?

Well, Sherlock also happens to be the name of the greatest detective who ever looked through a magnifying glass: Mr. Sherlock Holmes. And just like the great Mr. Holmes, I was born with a natural gift for solving mysteries.

SHERLOCK HOLMES

It may sound weird, but while most kids my age are busy doing homework, playing soccer, or scooping out their ear wax with paper clips,

I stay busy preparing myself for a life of mystery solving.

I've seen just about every detective movie ever made. I've seen the really good ones that keep you on the edge of your seat so much that you end up chewing off half your toenails without even realizing it. And I've also seen all the old black-and-white ones where everybody stands around talking so much that you wake up on the floor two hours later in a pool of your own drool.

But no amount of movie watching could have prepared

me for the Case of the Haunted Toolshed. Just hearing that name makes me feel like I have a pair of live squirrels in my stomach and two corks shoved up my nostrils . . . if you know what I mean. So bolt the doors, lock the windows, and remember to keep breathing as I tell you about my first official case as a private detective: Case #000001.

· Chapter Two ·
The Evening Caller?

I don't hear the doorbell at first.

It's Friday night and I'm in the bathroom trying to figure out why I can't get my Inspector Wink-Wink electric toothbrush to turn on. I can't hear much of anything because I'm too busy smacking my toothbrush against the side of the sink—which is basically how I try to fix most things.

My stubborn toothbrush does not respond.

So I bang it harder.

Inspector Wink-Wink is a cartoon show character that I like a lot. He's a detective, like me. But to be totally honest, it's really a show for younger kids. I'm probably one of the biggest Inspector Wink-Wink fans on the planet. But I try not to let anyone know because it's a little weird that I still like a little-kid show.

Before I realize what's happening, the top section with the brushing bristles pops off the base, bounces off the mirror, and falls into the toilet with a sickening little *ploop* sound. I watch in silent horror as it sinks into that nasty, dark cave at the bottom of the toilet bowl.

I freeze, clutch my forehead, and make a weird squeaking noise that sounds like someone just stepped on a hamster.

In the terrible silence that follows, just as

I hear the doorbell ring on its desperate third try, I notice that I've chipped the rim of the sink.

This makes me think of two important facts. Fact one: It's Friday night and my mom is out of town at my aunt Peachy's house in Phoenix (which is somewhere in Florida, I think). My aunt Peachy broke her clavicle, and my mom is staying with her for a few days to help take care of my creepy twin cousins. Fact two: My dad is sick in bed.

So I do what any kid would do in this situation when both his parents are unavailable:

I quickly cover up the sink's missing chunk with a gigantic blob of sparkly toothpaste.

"Mr. Asher is here and he wants to hire you!" my little sister, Hailey, exclaims, throwing open the bathroom door and nearly crushing all the delicate little bones in my right elbow with the doorknob.

"Aaaaaaaaaagh!" I groan like Frankenstein's monster as I roll around on the bathroom mat. I'm almost certain that my elbow bones have been crushed into a fine powder. For some unexplained reason, I can smell boiled cabbage—which can't be a good sign.

"Why do they call it a funny bone again?" I wheeze.

"Quit goofing around, Sherlock," she whispers. "Poor Mr. Asher looks like he's seen a ghost!"

Finally, my first official case as a private detective has arrived.

"Hi, Mr. Asher," I say when I find him in our living room.

"I'm sorry to bother you so late, Sherlock," he says, nervously fingering the handle of his cane.

Hailey is right. Mr. Asher looks freaked out. His eyes are all jumpy and bugged out, like he's a boxer who just got punched hard below the belt. Magnifying the problem are

10

his thick glasses, which make his eyes appear to be the size of white tennis balls. His face is covered in big gobs of sweat. His nose is making an eerie whistling noise.

"Sherlock, you must help us," he says between nose whistles. "There are strange things happening at the end of Baker Street. I may have . . . a poltergeist."

"I see," I say like any thoughtful detective would say, although I'm really thinking that I have absolutely no idea what "poltergeist" means.

"Cool, a poltergeist," Hailey says from behind me.

Great! My seven-year-old sister knows what he's talking about, but I don't have a clue. I make a mental note to brush up on my vocabulary.

"A poltergeist is a kind of ghost," Mr. Asher explains.

"Oh . . . I know that," I say like an idiot.

"My mother is visiting from the old country, and these strange events have made her very nervous," he continues. "Today she fainted three times, and now she's developed a terrible case of flatulence."

"Cool, flatulence," Hailey chirps.

What is everyone talking about?

"Flatulence?" I reply to Mr. Asher.

Hailey answers for him. "That means she's farting up a storm."

This case is not off to a great start.

Mr. Asher is a chunky, bald man who combs the wispy hair from the back of his head up and over his bald spot, which he then swirls around and around into a sort of hairy cinnamon roll.

"It started last night, with strange noises, like moaning and shrieking from another world," Mr. Asher explains as his nose whistle mysteriously changes key. "Then things start to disappear. Suddenly my mailbox is gone. Poof! My mother's fresh bundt cake is gone without a trace. Poof! Now even her glass eye is missing. Poof!"

"Cool, a glass eye," Hailey says excitedly.

I give her my best "shut up now" glare. But truthfully, the thought of Grandma

Asher's moist glass eye rolling around somewhere on a dusty carpet makes my stomach tighten into a fist.

"I think something evil has moved into my toolshed," Mr. Asher croaks in a way that no kid ever wants to hear an adult croak.

I'm waiting for Hailey to say, "Cool, something evil." But she doesn't.

In fact, the room gets quiet. Too quiet. I stare at Mr. Asher's magnified eyes. They slowly blink back at me, like twin garage doors opening and closing. Then even the tune he's been playing on his nose suddenly falls silent. It's so quiet in here you could hear a bug change its mind.

Then we hear it. A hollow, spine-straightening moan from another world. The evil spirits from beyond this life have followed Mr. Asher down the street from his house! The poltergeist is now in my house!

• Chapter Four •
That's the Spirit

The three of us remain frozen in mindless terror.

We strain to hear the sound again. Silence has never sounded so loud.

Then the groan returns. It's low and distant, like the sound a cow would make if a barn fell over on it.

Without warning, the evil spirit brushes my hand with its bony fingers! Blind with fear, I jump to my feet in a crouch. "Mommy!" I blurt out like a baby goat.

But then I look at my hand. It's not the evil spirit that has touched my hand at all. I'm still holding the base of my Inspector Wink-Wink toothbrush, which has finally sprung to life. It buzzes away cheerfully, obviously unaware that its top half remains at the bottom of the toilet.

I switch it off. But it keeps buzzing away. It is clearly in the off position, but it continues to buzz like mad. *Has the whole world gone bananas?* I wiggle it. I shake it. I finally whack it on the small table next to me. It goes quiet.

Just as I begin to feel relief, the rumbling groan returns. I look at Mr. Asher, who is now as white as a tub of sour cream.

"Um . . . that's just my dad, Mr. Asher," Hailey says calmly from behind me. "He probably can't reach his pain pills. I'll be right back." She runs through the kitchen and down the hallway to get my dad his pain pills.

I clear my throat while I try to think of something to say. "Mr. Asher," I begin with only a hint of a squeak, "I'll ask my dad if I can stay out late to work on this case. I'd like to help you get to the bottom of this mystery as quickly as possible. But I must warn you that my fee is ten dollars a day . . . or night."

I secretly hope that he says that my price is too high, calls me a dope, and storms out mumbling every bad word not in the dictionary.

But, of course, he doesn't. My luck is always like this.

"That sounds reasonable," he says, standing and edging closer to the door. "Sherlock, I've called the police, but they just laugh at me and I . . . I simply don't know where else to

turn." He looks around the room as if he doesn't remember how he even got here. "I've heard that you have a knack for solving mysteries. So please . . . just call me and let me know when you'll be arriving."

Before I can change my mind, he's out the door and fading into the inky darkness like a ghost with a limp.

I realize that I don't have his phone number. I realize I should have asked for more than ten dollars. And with a gasp, I realize I've made an ugly chip in the table with the base of my toothbrush.

I haven't even left the house yet and I've already damaged a sink, a table, and an elbow. I can't imagine how things could get any worse. . . .

Then I hear the toilet flush.

My toothbrush! The brushing bristles of my Inspector Wink-Wink toothbrush are gone forever! Tears creep into the corners of my eyes. My nose fills with snot. I even choke back a sob. (Hey, it was a collector's item!)

I'm struck with the uneasy feeling that this evening is only going to get worse.

· Chapter Five ·
Toe Jam

My dad's not sick in the traditional way, like someone with a stomach virus, a lung infection, or an armpit rash.

My dad had to stay home from work today because of something called gout. It's in his big toe.

Medically speaking, gout makes my dad's toe slightly swollen and the color of uncooked hamburger meat. Just the thought of his rotten toe makes me want to spew the entire contents of my stomach onto the carpet.

Our family doctor, Dr. Bell, says that gout happens to old guys like my dad when they stuff themselves with a lot of junk food while their wives are out of town. He says that a bunch of gross acid squirts out of the guy's liver or gizzard or something and gets sucked down to his toes by gravity.

I enter my dad's room slowly, staring at his big, ugly toe like it's about to explode and

spray toe jelly all over the room.

His toe now rises proudly out of the bedsheets, a shining example of everything that can go wrong with a foot.

"I need to help Mr. Asher with a mystery," I whisper to the toe.

"I heard," my dad answers from the other end of the bed.

"He thinks his house might be haunted," I say.

"Hailey told me all about it," he murmurs.

"Funny, huh?" I ask.

"Nothing is funny right now," he moans.

"Um . . . so I'm going to run down there and see if—"

"She tells me that Grandma Asher is farting up a storm," he interrupts.

"Well, that's not really part of the mystery," I reply quickly.

He laughs quietly. "Silent but deadly."

"What's that?" I ask.

"She wants to help you, Sherlock," he mutters.

"Grandma Asher wants to help me?" I ask.

"No. Hailey. Hailey wants to go with you, but I told her she can't," he says.

"I might be out pretty late," I say.

"Be back by nine o'clock," he mumbles.

"How about ten?" I ask, realizing that it's already seven-thirty.

"Nine o'clock sharp," he slurs. "And be very, very careful that your mother doesn't find out."

"Okay," I sigh, staring at the sad family of little piggies that live at the end of my dad's foot. I realize that after nine and a half years of life, I've never really taken a good look at my dad's toes. Now I know why. They look like they've been run over by a tank. Or a Zamboni.

"Have your toes always been bent like that?" I ask, trying to distract myself from the thought of what my mother would think of my after-hours detective work.

"It's rude to stare at a man's feet, son," he says.

"Dad, does this mean you're not taking me and Hailey to the circus tomorrow?" I ask, unable to take my eyes off his gnarled toes.

"Sorry, son," he says softly. "Maybe next year."

My dad starts to snore. I hope Hailey hasn't given him too many pain pills. He seems a bit loopy. I stare at his messed-up toes a bit longer, then stumble out into the hallway, holding my lurching stomach. As I close the door, I make a pledge that I will never take my normal-looking feet for granted again.

"Sherlock!" my older sister, Jessie, yells from the other end of the hall. "For some reason Mr. Asher is on the phone, and he's rambling on about how you better get over to his house fast."

• Chapter Six •
Sister Sledgehammer

"Hello?" I say, hoping Mr. Asher has called to say that it was all just a big mistake.

But the phone is dead. "Hello?" I say again just to make sure he's gone.

"Isn't it past your bedtime?" Jessie sneers while rolling her eyes. This is nothing new. She rolls her eyes whenever she communicates with anyone.

"Mr. Asher's up to his neck in weird stuff

tonight," I say, staring at the phone. "Dad says I can go and help him get to the bottom of things."

Jessie is thirteen years old and has been extremely moody since she turned eleven. She spends most of her time locked in her room practicing being angry.

Jessie's most favorite thing to do is to call her friends and talk about how miserable she is. Her second favorite thing to do is glare at me like I'm something stuck on the bottom of her shoe.

"You flushed the toilet, didn't you?" I ask, mostly to change the subject.

"Aaaghgh," she says again. "You've got a problem with that?" Another eye roll.

"Well, my toothbrush was in there," I explain.

This stops her dead in her tracks. She can't even roll her eyes. Her mouth drops open slightly.

"Um," I say, simply to break the uncomfortable silence. "It was my favorite toothbrush. A collector's item, actually. I was about to fish it out of there right before you flushed it."

"Aaaghgh," she gurgles, regaining her composure. She spins and storms off down the hall. She's almost running. I'm sure she's about to speed-dial all her friends to tell them that her freakish little brother now brushes his teeth in the toilet bowl.

But I must admit, that was the friendliest she's been in six months.

Suddenly I realize the phone is barking in alarm because I forgot to hang it up. And I'm still wearing my Inspector Wink-Wink slippers. Worse yet, I'm wasting time while poor Grandma Asher is floating so many air biscuits that every small bird in the neighborhood may be in danger.

"We haven't a moment to spare," I say to the empty kitchen. I'm not sure why I say this; it's just something Sherlock Holmes always says when he's late for a train.

It doesn't make me feel any better.

Because deep down inside, I know that I'm about to come face-to-face with my greatest fear in the world . . . the dark.

• Chapter Seven •
Howl

As I wait for my eyes to adjust to the darkness, the moon looks down at me like a giant panic button. Then it disappears, gobbled up by clouds.

"Sherlock!"

I flinch and spin around in my best kung fu fighting stance.

"Oh, please," Hailey snorts, coming out onto the porch. "You'd be better off just lying on the ground and playing dead."

"You almost gave me a heart attack," I grumble.

"You'll need this," she says, handing me a pink Girl Chat Sleepover backpack. (I lost my own backpack in an unfortunate fishing accident.) "And you'll need this," she says, clipping a matching Girl Chat Sleepover walkie-talkie to my belt.

"I can't wear this," I complain, holding up the backpack. "It's for girls."

"Listen, Sherlock," she says, waving a finger in my face. "This is the real deal. This is not a drill. This is not one of your dumb detective movies. So if Dad won't let me go with you, you're not leaving here with just a magnifying glass in your back pocket."

"Okay! Okay!" I surrender, pulling my arms through the thin straps of the daisy-covered backpack. "I just hope nobody sees me."

"It's packed with everything you might need," Hailey explains, looking me over. "Now you're fully equipped with a flashlight, your fingerprint kit, a whistle, a comb, a clean pair of underwear, twelve plastic bags for collecting evidence, a notepad, six pencils, a watch, and a compass."

"Please don't touch my underwear

ever again!" I exclaim. "That's gross."

"Oh, I also put some leftover crab cakes in there," she says, ignoring my concern for the privacy of my underwear drawer.

"I hate crab cakes," I protest.

"They're just a diversion in case you're attacked by a pack of hungry dogs," she explains.

I must admit I feel a little safer with the backpack on.

"Too bad it's such a spooky night," she says, peering up at the moon dodging in and out of the dark clouds. "Especially since you're the only kid I know who needs three night-lights."

"Do you think werewolves like crab cakes?" I ask, watching the moon.

"If you're not back by nine o'clock, we'll assume the worst has happened," she says.

Before I can chicken out, I begin walking toward the dark end of Baker Street.

· Chapter Eight ·
Red Leader

"Red Leader! This is Blue Fox! Do you copy? Over."

It's the walkie-talkie Hailey clipped to my belt. I'm only a few houses away, and she's already calling me.

"Hailey?" I ask while pushing down a little daisy-shaped button on the walkie-talkie.

"Red Leader! This is not a secure line. Do not use real names. I repeat, do not use real

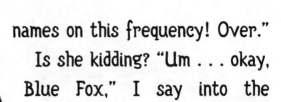

names on this frequency! Over."

Is she kidding? "Um . . . okay, Blue Fox," I say into the walkie-talkie. Geez, do I feel like an idiot.

"You forgot to say 'over'! Over!" blares the tiny voice amid a storm of static.

"Uh, okay . . . over," I say, trying to keep my voice down.

"Red Leader! What's your ten-twenty? Over!" Hailey's voice barks through the miniature speaker.

"What's that mean, Red Leader? Over," I say, looking around to make sure nobody is looking out their windows.

"Hey, *you're* Red Leader! I'm Blue Fox. Ten-twenty means your location. Over."

I'm getting a headache that's three miles

wide. "I just left! I'm only four houses away from our house, for goodness sake! Now leave me alone. Over and out." I clip the walkie-talkie back on my belt.

"Roger that, Red Leader!" Hailey's voice booms out into the night. "Have you used that extra pair of underwear yet?" she giggles.

I stop walking and turn the volume way down. "It's hard to get good help these days," I say to nobody in particular.

Now I know why the great Sherlock Holmes didn't use a walkie-talkie. You can't concentrate on the case at hand while someone is hollering at you all night about your supply of emergency underwear.

I pick up my pace, worried that I've just wasted valuable mystery-solving minutes yakking with the irritating Blue Fox.

Before long, I swear I hear the ragged breathing of bloodthirsty hounds in every shadow. I think I hear footsteps behind me. For some reason, I can smell my mom's beef stew with broccoli and lima beans—which is about as terrifying as it gets.

Just as my stomach starts twisting into a pretzel shape at the imagined odor of my mom's nasty beef stew . . .

I feel the trembling, bony fingers of the Grim Reaper as he rests his hand on my right shoulder, ready to pull me into the next world, kicking and screaming. Without thinking, I run for my life.

· Chapter Nine ·
Speed Demon

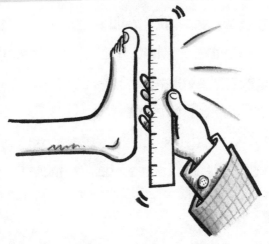

I may not be the smartest kid in my class, but I am the fastest.

By far.

In fact, I'm easily the fastest kid in my school. Maybe even the whole state. Don't ask me why. Even Dr. Bell says it makes no sense because I have such flat feet. They're so flat that whenever I step on a floor that my mom just mopped, my feet get stuck like two industrial-strength suction cups. My mom has to slide a spatula under each foot to free me. It's humiliating.

Except for solving mysteries and running like a greased pig shot out of a cannon, I'm usually pretty average.

But you should see me run.

Especially with the Grim Reaper on my tail.

My best friend, Lance, has a model of the Grim Reaper in his bedroom. It's one of those

PRESS FOR SCREAMING The Grim Reaper™
MADE IN CHINA

creepy things that I try not to think about, but the harder I try, the more I can't help but think about it. I hate that.

In case you've never heard of him, the Grim Reaper is a tall skeleton guy who floats around with a sword stuck to the end of a big walking stick. He wears a shabby old robe with a hood that's so big he can't possibly see who he is terrifying.

And then it hits me. . . .

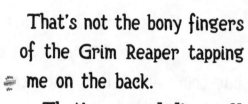

That's not the bony fingers of the Grim Reaper tapping me on the back.

That's my dad's cell phone vibrating in Hailey's Girl Chat Sleepover backpack! I come to a complete stop just one house away from Mr. Asher's house.

Hailey never mentioned putting the cell phone in the backpack. It must be her backup plan if the walkie-talkie doesn't work.

I yank the phone from the backpack and snap it open. "Hello?" I gasp.

"Sherlock, it's me!" Hailey exclaims. "Dad's gone. He's disappeared!"

· Chapter Ten ·
Toe Break

"How can a guy who can barely walk disappear?" I thunder into my dad's cell phone.

"How should I know!" Hailey yelps in exasperation. "You're the detective in the family."

I've seen a lot of Sherlock Holmes movies. Probably every one ever made. And one thing is for sure: he only dealt with one mystery at a time. Now I know why.

I think the great Mr. Holmes knew that when you try to think about two mysteries at once, your brain starts to melt like a stick of warm butter on the hood of an overheating car. It turns into sizzling butter goop.

"Where could he have possibly gone?" I ask. "To kick field goals? To stomp grapes? Maybe he suddenly decided to learn how to kickbox!"

"I thought he might be with you," she says.

"No, it's just me and the Grim Reaper out here," I mumble, looking up at the sky in frustration.

"Who's Jim Reaper?" she asks.

Why can't I just solve mysteries like a normal detective in the movies?

"Hailey," I say as calmly as I can after setting a new world record for sidewalk sprinting, "just look for him. Ask Jessie to help you. Let me know what you find out."

Hailey grunts in frustration. "Thanks for all your wonderful help. You're my hero!"

The phone goes silent in my ear.

I look up at the Ashers' house and silently wish for no more phone calls, footraces, or panic attacks.

I don't like my odds.

• Chapter Eleven •
Crime Scream

Mr. Asher might as well hang a sign that says, "GHOSTS WELCOME!"

The Asher home is located on a big plot of land at the very end of Baker Street. It leans a little to the left, so if you stare at it for too long you end up falling over like a guy with a serious inner-ear infection.

I begin to feel a little wobbly, so I'm careful not to stare at the house for longer than a few seconds at a time.

Looking at the Ashers' house makes me consider what motive someone might have for terrifying the Asher family.

"Motive" is a fancy word they use in detective movies. It means reason, but why they always have to use an uppity word like "motive" when "reason" would work just fine is something I haven't figured out yet. "So," I ask, "what *reason* would someone have to try to scare the people who live in this house?"

In detective movies, when the main guy is hired to investigate strange, weird, and ghostly-type stuff, it usually turns out to be the work of some bad guys wearing goofy ape costumes. These bad guys are always trying to scare an old couple off their property so they can build an eight-lane highway right where the couple's living room happens to be.

After you've seen a few hundred of these

movies, you learn one thing: Heroes almost always have a big chin.

I make a mental note to ask Mr. Asher if there's anyone who wants him to move off his property. If I can figure out a motive, I might get a jump on why these strange and unexplained things are happening.

Breaking down a puzzling mystery into simple steps like this is an important skill of the successful detective. It always makes me feel better.

But I don't feel better for long.

Because at that very moment, a thunderous, head-snapping roar blasts through the night air. My guts quiver. My lungs vibrate. My stomach feels like it's filled with three hundred nervous grasshoppers.

I secretly wish my chin were bigger.

· Chapter Twelve ·
Barf Bath

I cover my ears in front of
Mr. Asher's left-leaning, nail
bag of a house and I imagine that I'm
about to be snatched up into the jaws of a
Tyrannosaurus rex, flipped into the air like
a helpless rag doll, and swallowed whole
like a Swedish meatball.

But no dinosaur appears.

In fact, the earsplitting roar stops as

suddenly as it started.

Wait!

This is ridiculous. My imagination is out of control! I need to think clearly for once in my life!

Breathe in. Breathe out. Breathe in again. Relax.

Think. Think. *Think!*

What exactly am I dealing with here?

I smack my forehead a few times with my fist—which is how I try to get most things to start working properly.

Is this real? Is this some sinister plot cooked up to scare the Ashers? Or is this the work of something ghostly? I stroke my small chin as I consider the endless possibilities.

I feel in my bones that something is not right here. Or perhaps it's the smell of my own fear leaking out of my skin. Maybe I need that fresh pair of underwear.

Before I can figure out a suitable answer, the front door of the Ashers' home bangs open. "Sherlock! Please, come quick!" Mr. Asher hollers. "The ghost is back! There isn't a moment to lose!"

· Chapter Thirteen ·
Bundt Cakes and
Black Holes

Sniff...

As I stumble through the Ashers' door, I am struck by the sickening smell of raw terror in the air.

"That's not a Girl Chat Sleepover back-pack, is it?" Mr. Asher asks.

I can't seem to think of an answer to his question. There are too many alarm bells going off in my head. The foul smell from outside is also in Mr. Asher's house! It

doesn't take long to realize what's going on:
I've walked right into Grandma Asher's gas
problem! It's a choking haze that I can only
describe as a mixture of vinegar, spoiled milk,
hard-boiled eggs, and burned meat loaf.

I grab Mr. Asher's shoulder to steady
myself. "Silent but deadly, indeed," I gasp.

I consider the very real possibility that if
someone were to strike a match, the Ashers'

house might erupt into an enormous ball of flames. The explosion could quite possibly take out the entire neighborhood. Maybe even some nearby towns. Heck, this side of the Earth could vanish altogether.

It's at this point things get a little blurry. I hear nervous voices. I sense chaos. I see Mrs. Asher walking down the hallway wearing strands of garlic around her neck and what appear to be asparagus tips in her ears. My eye stops on Grandma Asher coming through the swinging door to the dining room. My eyes widen as I realize that she is winking at me— No! Not winking . . . she just hasn't found her missing eye yet!

Only after leaning over the sink to place my trembling nostrils as close to the open kitchen window as possible, I slowly, carefully assemble the important details of what is quickly becoming my living nightmare.

The loud, thundering roars happen about every hour or so. Shortly after Mrs. Asher's first bundt cake disappeared, Grandma Asher baked another bundt cake to replace it. It disappeared, too, from the windowsill above the sink. Grandma Asher's glass eye was left near the cake to keep an eye on it. That plan didn't work. Most troubling, there are still strange banging noises coming from the toolshed in the far corner of Mr. Asher's property.

"Uh . . . what's a bundt cake?" is all I can think to ask.

"You've never had bundt cake?" Grandma Asher asks with a wide, unbelieving eye. "Sit

down, young man, and I'll make another one and show you."

"Enough!" explodes Mr. Asher. "No more bundt cakes! Three bundt cakes in one night are more than any man can take!" he cries, shaking his cane at the ceiling.

"Mr. Asher, I'm going to have a look around the property," I gag. I manage to make it onto the front porch. I stagger down the steps and out toward the street.

Suddenly, and without any kind of warm-up, my ankle sends out shock waves of eye-popping pain. I've stepped on a bear trap! Or an alligator has just taken a free sample of my ankle! Maybe I've been attacked by a rat the size of a bowling ball!

I crumple to the ground. The jolt of pain is so unexpected and shocking, it's all I can do not to wet my pants.

"I see you've discovered the hole from

which my new mail-
box was uprooted,"
Mr. Asher calls
out from the porch.

"Yes!" I wheeze
like an accordion
being sat on by
Santa Claus.

"You're not resting already, are you?" Mr.
Asher asks suspiciously.

"No," I rasp, pulling the throbbing remains
of my left leg out of the hole. The pain is so
great that I'm amazed to see my foot is still
attached to the bottom of my leg. "How long
did you have your mailbox before it was
stolen?" I manage to ask.

"Let's see," Mr. Asher says, banging the
cane several times on the wooden porch. "I
just installed it this past Wednesday. It was

gone by Friday. It was a beauty. It even had a brass flag."

"Interesting," I say, although I'm really trying to figure out if I'll ever be able to walk again.

"Honestly, Sherlock, I'm a little more concerned about the ruckus coming from my toolshed."

"I'm sure you are!" I sputter. Boy, can't the guy just let me suffer in peace?

I need an aspirin the size of a truck tire.

"Mr. Asher," I say, struggling into a sitting position, "I must continue my investigation because my time is running short."

I feel my dad's cell phone vibrate urgently in my pocket. What now?

Little do I know that my case and my luck are about to take a turn for the worse.

"**D**id you find Dad?" I ask, flicking open the phone.

"What do you mean? Where's your father?"

It's my mom! She's must be calling from Aunt Peachy's house.

"Uh . . . hi, Mom," I say cheerfully. "How's Aunt Peachy's clarinet?"

"The word is 'clavicle,' Sherlock," she says sternly. "Don't play dumb with me."

"Who's playing?" I say defensively.

"Why are you answering your father's cell phone?" she asks.

"Um . . . because it started vibrating?"

"And why doesn't anyone answer the house phone?" she asks.

"Jessie's hogging the phone to tell the whole world that I brush my teeth with toilet water," I answer.

"And just what did you mean when you asked me if I found Dad?"

"What do you mean what did I mean?" I say stupidly, mostly because I can't think of anything else to say.

As my luck would have it, another thunderous moan fills the air surrounding the Ashers' property. The groaning roar is so loud I think I might get a nosebleed. Like before, it stops after about a minute.

"FOR HEAVEN'S SAKE, WAS THAT YOUR

FATHER?" my mom hollers on the other end of the phone. "WHAT ON EARTH HAVE YOU CHILDREN DONE TO HIM!"

"No! Mom! Wait! That wasn't Dad! That was just an evil spirit or something. I swear. . . . In fact, we can't even find Dad."

"Can't find him? He can't even walk. How could you lose your father?" she asks so loudly that I have to hold the phone a few inches from my ear.

"We didn't exactly lose him," I explain. "He just sort of vanished into thin air. Poof!"

"Your father poofed?" she blurts out, like she can't believe what she's hearing.

"Are you telling me someone has kidnapped your father?" she shouts.

"Kidnapped?" I sputter. "I never said. . . . " This conversation is getting out of hand. I need to get control of this situation or I'll be grounded until I'm a grandfather. "No, Mom.

I don't think he's been kidnapped," I say calmly into the phone. "Although I can't be sure . . . because I'm not at home."

"I'm taking the next flight home!" my mom exclaims, but not to me. I think she's talking to Aunt Peachy. She's in full panic mode.

"Sherlock, stay where you are. And stay away from the toilet!" The phone goes dead in my ear.

It's at that moment I notice an enormous, strange van. The van jerks to a stop. Searching eyes stare at me from the passenger-side window.

• Chapter Fifteen •
Strangers in a Strange Land

"Nice backpack, kid," a deep, grumbly voice says from the darkened passenger-side window of the van.

I gulp.

"You better get home and avoid the street tonight," says Mr. Deep Voice.

The van rolls slowly past and into the darkness. I watch the two taillights fall away into the mist like the red eyes of a dragon.

"You're not the boss of me," my voice peeps. I want to sound tough and brave, but I sound more like a nervous guinea pig.

Who was that? Why were their headlights off? Could they be the ones trying to scare the Ashers off their property? Were they trying to scare me off my first official case as a private detective?

"The plots thickens," I say to nobody, although I'm really thinking that if the plot thickens any more it'll start to feel like quicksand.

I feel goose bumps crawl across my back, skitter up my neck, and spread across my scalp like a herd of spiders.

I remember something that my dad is always telling me: "Son, there is nothing to fear but fear itself."

This really drives me nuts.

The truth is, when you're really scared you can't think about anything. Your body simply switches into autopilot and starts growing goose bumps like crazy. So in order to keep myself from looking like a plucked chicken all night, I decide to get organized.

I pull out the pencil and pad of paper Hailey put in the backpack. To organize my thoughts I make a list of the many puzzling facts of this case.

I read my list over. I realize I've simply organized my confusion. I pull Hailey's Girl Chat Sleepover flashlight out of the backpack. I stagger across Mr.

Asher's lawn and turn the corner. I lower my smallish chin, determined to make a major break in the case, goose pimples or no goose pimples.

One clue. One footprint. One trace of evidence is all I need. No detective likes going home empty handed. And neither do I.

Of course, the one clue I do end up finding is so shocking, so unexpected, it will change the way I think about fingers forever.

• Chapter Sixteen •
Can I See a Show of Hands?

"Red Leader. This is Blue Fox. Do you copy? Over."

I forgot about the Girl Chat Sleepover walkie-talkie. Although I turned down the volume, Hailey's voice is loud enough to make me jump.

"Did you find Dad?" I ask hopefully.

"Uh, that's a negative, Red Leader. Please refer to that person as Hot Skunk for the remainder of the mission. Over!"

"Hot Skunk? You've got to be kidding me!" I holler.

"Uh, that's a negative. Over!" Hailey's faint voice replies.

"Is Jessie helping you look for him?" I ask.

"That's a big negative, Red Leader. Happy Fish is not participating in Operation Hot Skunk Rescue. Over."

"Happy Fish?" I growl into the phone. "Operation Hot Skunk Rescue? Hailey, I don't have time for this!"

"Please don't use real names on this freq—"

I turn the thing off before she can finish.

I'm convinced that my little sister is not good for my mental health. I clip the walkie-talkie back onto my belt.

Putting as little pressure as possible on my ballooning ankle, I teeter over to the area under the Ashers' kitchen window.

I sweep the pink beam of light from the Girl Chat Sleepover flashlight across the ground, looking for any sign of a trespasser. But instead of the footprints I expect to find in the soft dirt under the window, I discover handprints. Deep prints made by long, super size hands with fingers as thick as sausages. Gross! I move the pink circle of light back and forth on the ground, but there are only handprints. Not one footprint? That's odd.

Handprints? Why would someone walk on their hands like an acrobat to steal bundt cakes

and a glass eye? So they wouldn't leave
fingerprints? So their face wouldn't be seen?
Or maybe they couldn't walk on their feet. . . .

"NO! It can't be!" I croak.

I clutch my forehead as if to pull the hunch
from my mind. But it just grows and spreads
and blossoms like all the weeds in our front
yard. There's no escaping it. . . .

The thief could quite possibly be my dad!

• Chapter Seventeen •
Calling for Backup

It all seems to fit.

My dad is missing. He can't walk on his feet. He's been moaning like a ghost because of his gout-infested toe. He's been acting goofy. And he's been eating like a vacuum since he dropped Mom off at the airport . . . and I think he likes bundt cake, too.

Despite the cool, misty air, I start to sweat like a pig in a blanket.

With a jolt of panic, I wrestle the phone from my pocket and punch in the phone number of the one person who can handle something this big. The person who will always stand by me no matter how bad things get.

"Da," I hear Lance's grandmother say after the first ring.

"Hello, Grandma Peeker! Sorry to call this late . . . anyway, I'm wondering if Lance can—"

"Who is this?" Grandma Peeker interrupts.

"Oh, sorry . . . this is Sherlock," I say. "Um . . . I know it's late, but this may be a matter of life or—"

The phone bangs down like it's been dropped from the roof of a skyscraper. Whatever happened to phone manners?

Lance's grandma is odd. She's short with wide, wiggly arms. She has a drooping, gumdrop-size wart just under her right eye that I try not to look at, but the more I try not to look at it the more I do. I hate that. She smells like old cheese.

"Hiya, Sherlock!" Lance finally says on the other end of the line.

I clear my throat. "Would you like your milk in a bag?"

"What?" Lance asks.

"Would you like your milk in a bag?" I repeat slowly.

"Huh? Sherlock, did you bang your head on something?"

"Would you like your milk in a bag?" I say louder.

"What on earth are you talking about?" he asks.

"WOULD YOU LIKE YOUR STINKING MILK IN A BAG?" I shout.

Lance is quiet for a few moments. I can hear him breathing. "Have you gone completely crazy?" he asks finally.

"No! You knucklehead!" I holler into the phone. "That's our secret code!"

"Secret code?" he asks, like he's never heard those two words said together before.

"Yes! The secret code that means you're supposed to drop everything and come running because your best friend in the whole world needs you! The secret code that we were always going to remember for the rest of our lives!"

"I don't remember making any secret code with you," he says.

"What good is an emergency secret code if the only other guy who knows it can't remember it? Just forget that I called."

"Well, since you got me out of the bath, you might as well tell me what your big secret-code emergency is all about."

"I need you to come and help me on a case," I say, shaking my head because I already know what his answer will be.

"At this hour?" he snorts. "You *are* crazy. Besides, I just put on my pajamas."

"C'mon, Lance! I need you on this one," I beg.

"Sorry, pal, but we're about to watch the

final episode of *Bug Chompers*," he says. "It's the major television event of the season."

I close the phone on Lance and his bug show. He's my best friend, but I'm beginning to think he's allergic to doing anything without a remote control in his hand.

My dad's cell phone starts vibrating again in my pocket. Oh, brother. Could this night possibly get any worse?

Before I can answer that question, someone rushes up from behind me, grabs Hailey's Girl Chat Sleepover backpack, and starts to run.

Sadly, I'm still strapped to the dang thing.

• Chapter Eighteen •
Close Encounter

If being dragged backward through the mud on your butt were an Olympic sport, I would surely win a gold medal.

I raise my arms up like I'm being robbed and slip out of the backpack's straps. I look back for an instant and see Hailey's backpack being carried off into the darkness by a short, burly man wearing a big fur coat.

Wild with panic, I sprint for my life.

I crash through thorny bushes. I hurdle neatly trimmed hedges. I scamper through Mr. Alessandri's army of lawn gnomes. Not bad for a lame duck!

The next thing I know, my right foot knocks the head off a cement garden bunny and I'm belly surfing. I scramble across Mrs. Egan's shadowy lawn and nearly knock myself silly when I whack my head on a low-hanging bird feeder. I almost suffer a severe panic attack when I become entangled in someone's garden hose. Worst of all, I can smell boiling cabbage again.

Midway through my mad dash down the obstacle course that is Baker Street, I see the mysterious van again. This time I notice that there is a large painting of a ferocious lion on the side of the van. Before I can figure out

exactly what that means, I am spotted. "Hey,
kid!" Mr. Deep Voice shouts. But I keep moving.
If dogs don't like me, I can only image what a
van full of ferocious lions will think of me.

By the time I reach my front porch, I am

completely out of steam. I flop onto my back, gasping.

I begin to relax. I am safe. I will not need an ambulance.

As the night's disturbing events begin to flutter through my mind, the screen door swings open and almost smashes my head down into my neck.

"AAAGHGH!" I scream, curling up in a ball and grabbing my head.

"What the . . . Dad, is that you?" Hailey gasps.

The porch light snaps on and I am blinded.

"Oh, it's just you," she says, clearly disappointed. "Whoa, you look like something even a cat wouldn't drag in."

"Thanks," I sputter, checking my flattened skull for missing pieces.

"I've been calling you and calling you. Why haven't you answered?" she asks.

I suddenly realize that during all the

running, jumping, dragging, and head smashing, I've lost my dad's cell phone. "I don't have it."

"It's probably in the backpack," she says, looking around.

"I lost that, too," I say.

"And my walkie-talkie?" she asks.

I look down at my belt. The walkie-talkie is gone also. "You may want to try the area around Mrs. Egan's bird feeder," I moan.

"What kind of detective loses more things than he finds?" she says, crossing her arms.

"The three of you have a good point," I groan as my blurry vision turns my little sister into triplets.

"What if that fresh pair of underwear ends up in the wrong hands?" she asks, just trying to irritate me. "Well, the cops are on their way here to find out what happened to Hot Skunk, so if you don't want to get blamed for everything, you better find him fast."

"The police?" I blurt out, leaping to my feet and waiting for my eyes to stop spinning in their sockets. "Dad's not lost; he's just misplaced," I say, pushing my way into the house.

Jessie sighs behind me. "This family's getting weirder by the minute."

· Chapter Nineteen ·
Spilling the Beans

Just as I thought, the location of my dad turns out to be not much of a mystery after all.

Two minutes into my search, I try the backyard. I hear him before I see him. He's snoring somewhere in the backyard like a gas-powered chain saw. I find him sleeping underneath the cushion on one of our reclining patio chairs.

I return to the house and start digging

through our kitchen's many junk drawers for a flashlight. I find six flashlights, but none of them work. Then I remember my Inspector Wink-Wink battery-operated night-lights.

I return to the backyard and quietly check my dad's hands for mud or dirt that could link him to the Ashers' property. He's clean. Whew! That's a relief. I feel a little tug of guilt for even suspecting him in the first place.

The relief I feel at solving this mini-mystery makes me realize how much the mystery at the Ashers' house has shaken my confidence. Even worse, it's almost nine o'clock. As any good detective knows, almost all mysteries that can be solved are solved within the first few hours. My case is getting cold. And so is my dad; his hands feel like a pair of frozen dinners.

I get Jessie off the phone to help with my dad. Not surprisingly, she's annoyed at the

interruption. "Nice night-light, Detective Dimwit," she says. "Are you wearing matching diapers?" My sister is just a laugh a minute.

We certainly can't lift him. And we can't seem to wake him, either. So Jessie and I roll my dad back into the house on the patio chair's two creaking wooden wheels.

"Easy! Easy up that step, people!" Hailey commands, acting like she's in charge of us. "Lift from the knees, not from the back. Get your head in the game, Sherlock. Look alive, Jessie!"

We leave Dad and his rolling patio chair parked in the center of the family room. I tell Hailey that she can't give him any more pain medication until tomorrow.

"He sounds like he might sleep until Halloween anyway," Hailey says.

"I'm calling Mom," Jessie announces, marching out of the room. "She needs to know that I've got everything under control." Moments later her bedroom door slams shut.

I shake my head. "Boy, I'd like to be a fly in the ointment," I say.

Hailey laughs. "I think you mean a fly on the wall. Sherlock, you look like you were on the wrong end of an avalanche."

"You wouldn't believe the half of it."

"Step into my office, big brother," she says, pulling me down the hall to her room.

For some reason, I tell Hailey everything about my case. It just comes pouring out. The farting granny. The vanishing bundt cakes. The missing mailbox. The runaway eye. The chunky handprints. The burly backpack thief.

Even the giant van with the lions on the side. "There are two hundred pieces to this puzzle, and none of them seem to fit together," I grumble.

"Is there anything else?" she asks.

"Isn't that enough?" I ask. "Oh . . . I also shortened a cement bunny."

I don't think she's really listening. She bites her lip. She nods. She taps her chin a few times. She looks as if she's trying to figure out whether my head will ever return to its original shape.

"I think I know what you've been overlooking," she finally says.

"You do?" I exclaim, sitting up straight.

Before Hailey can say anything else, Jessie sticks her head into the room and giggles. "Uh, Sherlock, there's an Officer Lestrade at the door about Dad. But he also wants to ask you something about a broken garden bunny."

Hailey's eyes grow two sizes. "I thought you were kidding."

· Chapter Twenty ·
Lightning Strikes

"Holy fandango!" Hailey whispers so loud she might as well be yelling. "We forgot about the cops! We're surrounded! Quick, hide in my hamper!"

I narrow my eyes at Jessie. "Tell Officer Lestrade to have a seat. We'll be right out."

Jessie snickers. "Then I'll call Mom. She's gonna love this."

Once the door clicks shut, I turn back to Hailey.

"Well?" I say.

"Well what?" she whispers back.

"C'mon, Hailey! You were just about to tell me what I've overlooked."

"I was?" she replies.

"HAILEY!"

"Okay! Okay!" she says. "Let's see. . . . Oh, I was going to say that you need to stop looking for connections and figure out what's *not* connected."

"Is that supposed to be helpful?" I ask.

"Yes!" she says, standing up straight and lifting her chin. "You've made the mistake of trying to put things together when you should be taking them apart."

I jump to my feet. "I might go to prison in a few minutes for kicking the head off a lawn ornament! You can't do any better than that?"

"You may have more than just *one* mystery on your hands. Don't you see? There may be lots of strange things going on at Mr. Asher's house, but that doesn't mean they're all connected in some way. Get it? Your mailbox mystery may have nothing to do with the missing cakes. The vanishing eye may not be caused by whoever is haunting Mr. Asher's toolshed. The men in the weird van—"

"Wait a minute!" I interrupt. "That's good.

Really good. Gooder than good. That's the goodest."

It's like I've gotten an eight-hundred-pound monkey off my back. Hailey has handed me the key that I've been missing, and now I'm unlocking all the doors in my head.

"What are you doing?" Hailey asks from behind me.

I yank the cord that lifts her window shades, throw open the window, and lift the screen out of its frame. As I hand Hailey the screen, I pull her chair over to the window.

"Hailey, I think I can help Mr. Asher get to the bottom of things. And I've still got eight minutes until the clock strikes nine," I say, nodding at her Girl Chat Sleepover wall clock. "So stall Officer Lestrade for just five minutes and then tell him to meet me down the street at Mr. Asher's house."

"Stall him?" she sputters. "With what?

Dad's stamp collection?"

"Think of something," I say as I swing my legs out of her window. "Maybe show him Dad's toes. If that doesn't distract him, nothing will."

"Have you lost your mind, Sherlock?" she asks, running to the open window.

But I'm already long gone.

• Chapter Twenty-one •
I Got Your Poof
Right Here!

"**W**ow! Did someone attack you with a rowing oar?"

Mr. Asher is looking at me through the peephole in his front door.

"Could you please open the door, Mr. Asher?"

"Oh, sorry," he says with a nervous laugh. Finally the door opens. I push past him, limp directly into the kitchen, and start flinging

open every drawer.

"Sherlock, what are you doing?" he asks above the clatter of kitchen drawers opening and closing.

"What is this called?" I demand to know, holding up a silver cooking utensil that claps together at the end.

I see fear flicker in his eyes as he stares at the cooking tool I'm snapping open and closed like a metallic crab claw.

"Those are called tongs." The voice comes from Mrs. Asher, who has quietly entered the kitchen.

Her eyes dart back and forth between her husband and me. She slowly picks up a meat thermometer from one of the open drawers. I think she plans to use it to protect her husband in case I attack him with the clacking tongs.

Instead I step over to the sink and go to work. The Ashers are silent behind me. I can feel their eyes on the back of my neck.

"Don't make any sudden movements," Mrs. Asher whispers to her husband.

"He may have had his brains scrambled," Mr. Asher whispers back. "It looks like someone took batting practice with his head."

"Look at this!" I announce suddenly, spinning around wildly. They both gasp in alarm. They gasp again when their eyes follow my outstretched arm and come to rest on the single glass eye clasped firmly in the end of the silver tongs.

"How did you . . . " Mr. Asher's voice trails off before he can finish.

"I fished it out of the garbage disposal," I explain, dropping the eye into a glass of water that's half empty. "I could only hope that you didn't need to use the garbage disposal before I could return tonight. Luckily, you didn't. It was the only logical place it could be, since someone who was stealing fresh-baked bundt cakes would have no use for a glass eye."

"That's amazing," says Mrs. Asher.

"I figure it rolled off the windowsill when the second cake was being stolen," I explain. "I simply imagined the places it could be, and decided that it must have rolled down the drain."

"Brilliant," says Mr. Asher with a tap of his cane.

I smile. "Just wait until I show you what happened to your mailbox. Follow me!"

• Chapter Twenty-two •
You've Got No Mail!

"Mr. Asher, exactly where was your garbage can this past Thursday night?"

"Don't tell me you think my garbage can ate my new mailbox," Mr. Asher says, pointing at the black hole with his cane.

"Am I standing about where you left your garbage can last Thursday night?" I ask, placing my feet on top of the curb.

"Yes. Yes, that is where I left it," he

insists, as if he's being accused of something. "And that is where it was the next day when I discovered my mailbox was missing."

I snap my fingers so suddenly Mr. Asher flinches. "Don't you see, Mr. Asher? Your mailbox was taken by accident when your garbage was picked up early Friday morning. It's at the Baskerville Municipal Dump right now under tons of dirty diapers, moldy bread, and uneaten beef stew with broccoli and lima beans."

"That's impossible," he says gruffly. "Why would the garbageman take my new mailbox?"

"The garbageman doesn't actually lift up these new garbage cans," I say. "You see, it's all robotic. Our garbage cans are grabbed by a giant pair of robotic pinchers that reach out from the side of the truck, like a pair of garbage-grabbing pliers. They hoist the cans up and dump the junk in the back of the truck."

Mr. Asher stares at me with a blank face. "I'm usually in bed at that hour, so I would never have noticed," he mumbles.

"You installed your new mailbox too close to where you leave your garbage can. The two-fingered clampers must have reached around your garbage can and yanked your new mailbox up with your garbage can."

"It had a lovely brass flag," Mr. Asher says with a sniff.

"I'm sorry for your loss, Mr. Asher," I say, patting him on the shoulder. "Now, if you'll follow me, it's time to unmask the person who's behind the haunting of your toolshed."

• Chapter Twenty-three •
Off to the
Wheelbarrow Races

I'm so excited by the sudden turnaround of luck that I never even see the wheelbarrow until it's too late.

Just as I think I'm on a roll that would even make Sherlock Holmes green with envy, I'm suddenly belly surfing for the second time tonight. Only this time I'm left with about four tablespoons of dirt in my mouth.

It takes me a few moments to realize

exactly what has happened. And why I'm eating a dirt sandwich.

I roll onto my knees and do my best to spit the soil from my mouth.

That's when I hear Mr. Asher crashing through some tall bushes to my right. "Mr. Asher," I whisper as loud as I can, "I'm over here." I hear him stop and grunt, but he moves on toward the toolshed without me.

But wait! That's not him. Mr. Asher can't be on my right. Because I now see him stumbling out of the darkness from behind me. And he doesn't see the wheelbarrow, either.

What a dumb place to leave a wheelbarrow! Before I can move out of the way, Mr. Asher trips and plows into me like a bull in a china shop.

"Ooooomph!" Mr. Asher wheezes, while at the same time blowing an alarmingly high-pitched blast from his nose whistle.

I'm knocked like a circus clown into two backward somersaults.

"Sherlock?" Mr. Asher groans. "Sorry, I didn't see you."

"No problem," I squeak.

With some panic, I realize that my lungs no longer work.

I think I've been hit in the solar plexus. I know this because Lance once told me that your solar plexus is a small section of your guts, right above your stomach and below your rib cage, that acts like an emergency shut-off button for your lungs. Well, my lung button has taken a direct hit. Unfortunately, Lance never mentioned where the emergency restart button is. My lungs feel like two tiny raisins dangling helplessly next to my heart. I can smell boiling cabbage again. *What does that mean!*

Finally, my raisins reinflate. I suck in the cool air. I look over to make sure Mr. Asher is okay. In the darkness I can see he is standing again, his hands on his knees.

But about forty yards behind him, I see two

flashlights coming through the brush.

Officer Lestrade! He's too early! I'm so close to solving this mystery I can taste it— no, wait . . . that must be the dirt sandwich.

"Quick, Mr. Asher," I plead, steering him by the arm so he doesn't see the flashlights coming our way. "Let's finish this haunted toolshed business once and for all."

"Sherlock, I need to rest," he insists.

"You there, wait!" thunders a voice from behind us.

"Quick, Mr. Asher, take a rest in this wheelbarrow!" I shout.

"**W**ho's that?" Mr. Asher asks in a shaky voice as he bounces around in the wheelbarrow.

"I've called for backup," I huff as I crazily wheel Mr. Asher over the bumpy, uneven ground. "We must make it back to the toolshed."

"Slow down!" he calls back to me. "I think I just swallowed my gum!"

Mr. Asher's property stretches from Baker

Street all the way back to Highway 67 and the fairgrounds. I'm sure those men in the van have their own evil plans for using this giant piece of property to make a fortune. Maybe as the site of a new football stadium. Or a skyscraper factory. Possibly a long-term parking lot for blimps.

"There it is," Mr. Asher says, pointing to the dark shape of his toolshed.

I dump Mr. Asher out of the wheelbarrow like a heavy load of chopped wood. There's no sign of the flashlights that were so close behind us. We've lost them. But they can't be far away.

"C'mon," I whisper to Mr. Asher as I walk past him and approach the door of the toolshed as quietly as a cat with slippers on.

I take a deep breath, pull my night-light from my pocket, and kick the door open with a bang.

"That's not an Inspector Wink-Wink night-light, is it?" Mr. Asher whispers over my shoulder.

"Don't move, cake stealers!" I squeak, careful not to enter the toolshed while at the same time cursing my guinea pig-like voice.

My nose detects something I'm not familiar with. A sickening, sour smell not unlike the smell of a wet dog. I want to enter the toolshed and have a look around, but I'd feel better with something to protect myself.

"Mr. Asher," I whisper, reaching behind me, "can I borrow your cane for a minute?"

He simply huffs in reply.

"Please, Mr. Asher, I'll be careful," I say.

He snorts like he thinks I'm nuts. Without taking my eyes off the door of the toolshed, I reach back farther and tap him on the arm of his wool coat.

Wait . . . I don't remember any wool coat when we left the house.

I spin around and raise my Inspector Wink-Wink night-light . . . revealing the face of an enormous, orange-haired monster whose sickening breath carries just the slightest hint of crab cakes.

• Chapter Twenty-five •
The Beast

"Nice doggie," I peep.

It's all I can think to say. Although the monster standing before me is more like a hairy refrigerator than any dog.

My night-light reveals the monster's heart-stopping face. Yikes!

Going numb with fear, I drop the night-light. It bounces off my grapefruit-size ankle and lands in the grass. The beast is now a large, dim outline against a distant street-light. I look down and see that the light now reveals the beast's feet, which are actually more like hands than feet.

Remaining motionless, I realize that I've solved my mystery. This is the thief I've been looking for. A thief who walks on his hands.

"Edward!" a gruff voice calls. I see flash-lights coming near us from the direction of the voice.

"Uh . . . I'm Sherlock, not Edward," my voice quivers.

"Not you, kid," the voice says. "I'm talking to Edward."

I'm struck dumb by the idea that someone would actually name a monster Edward.

Edward moves off happily toward the voice, which I now recognize as the voice from the big van with the lion painted on the side. The beast hugs Mr. Deep Voice and a young woman who is with him.

It's at this moment I realize what I'm looking at. "It's an orange monkey," I say out loud, although I meant to say that to myself.

"This is Edward," laughs the woman. "He's not a monkey; he's a Bornean orangutan. We're from the circus. When we came into town last night and started setting up our tents, Edward wandered off. We've been searching for him ever since. I hope he hasn't caused too much trouble."

Of course, an orangutan! Suddenly everything starts to make sense.

But why Edward? Who came up with that name? It seems like a huge, ugly orangutan should have a name that fits, like Kong, or Sampson, or Big Red.

"He's a regular escape artist," laughs Mr. Deep Voice, handing Edward a mango.

"FREEZE!" a voice off to my right shouts. "NOBODY MOVE!"

"It's okay, Officer Lestrade," I shout into the darkness. "It's just an orangutan."

"A what?" Mr. Asher shrieks from the direction of Officer Lestrade.

"It's just Edward," I say with a croak. "From the circus. Not to worry, Mr. Asher. The final piece of your mystery has just fallen into place." Boy, I like the sound of that.

"He's no harm to anyone," shouts Mr. Deep Voice, handing another mango to Edward.

"Wait until the guys back at the station hear this one," Officer Lestrade laughs nervously. He slowly approaches our weird little nighttime gathering, never taking his eyes off Edward.

"I'm so glad you're not hurt, Sherlock," Mr. Asher says, stepping into the light. "I'm sorry I left you. When you kicked open that door, I guess I got spooked. I thought I'd better bring in some reinforcements."

I smile. "All in a day's work, Mr. Asher. Or a night's work. Now I need someone to call my mom, or I'm going to have to run away with the circus."

I can't help but feel proud of myself.

I've done it. I've solved my first official case as a detective. And a tough one. Hailey was right. This case was really a mystery, wrapped in a puzzle, stuffed in a coincidence.

Everyone congratulates me on my "nerves of steel." Mr. Deep Voice hands me five free tickets to the circus tomorrow. Mr. Asher hands me a check made out to "Sherlock."

Edward hands me a mango.

Officer Lestrade says he's going to recommend me for an Outstanding Citizen Award from the Baskerville Board of Supervisors. I'm just glad he's forgotten about the headless bunny in all the excitement.

I learn from Mr. Deep Voice that the howls and roars we've been hearing are actually "long calls," a male orangutan's way of establishing his new territory. The backpack stunt is a trick Edward performs with Kreepy the Clown in the circus. And the bundt cake? Who knows? Probably just an orangutan's curiosity, since Edward prefers fresh fruit over cakes and pastries.

Mr. Asher hurries inside to spread the good news and to call my mom at my aunt Peachy's house. He promises to explain how I saved the day. And night.

Looking back, I realize that I should have

known that the prints I found under Mr. Asher's window were not from a human. It seems so obvious now that I could kick myself. But I can't complain. My orangutan mystery made the front page of the metro section in the *Baskerville Daily News*. And I hung the Outstanding Citizen Award certificate from the Baskerville Board of Supervisors on my wall, right above the photo of me, Hailey, Lance, Grandma Peeker, and Mr. Asher at the circus with Edward the Orangutan and Kreepy the Clown.

There are only two questions that I'm unable to answer at this point:

What's with the boiling cabbage smell? And . . .

Will Mr. Alessandri hire me to find out who broke his cement bunny?

Only time will tell.

In the meantime, I'll keep studying my library of Sherlock Holmes movies, so I'm ready for whatever mystery comes knocking at my door next.

Introducing Joe Sherlock, Kid Detective!

Case #000001:
The Haunted Toolshed
Hc 0-06-076189-X
Pb 0-06-076188-1

Case #000002:
The Neighborhood Stink
Hc 0-06-076187-3
Pb 0-06-076186-5

Case #000003:
The Missing Monkey-Eye Diamond
Hc 0-06-076191-1
Pb 0-06-076190-3

Joe Sherlock was born with a fear of the dark, an allergy to peanut butter, and a natural gift for solving mysteries.

Read all the books in the series and find out whether the weird, bizarre, and embarrassing will stump this great kid detective.